Chelsea's New Home

To Jessica Brooke,
Welcome to the world!
Trust in your heart!
Kimberley Levy

By Kimberley M. Levy
Illustrated by Terry Herman

PRINTSTAR
BOOKS ★

Affiliated Publishers
Milwaukee • Denver • Vancouver, B.C.

www.chelseasnewhome.com

Illustrations by Terry Herman
Cover and Text Design by Shelby Keefe

05   04   03   02   01   5 4 3 2 1

ISBN: 0-9706531-2-3
Library of Congress Card Number: 2001086177
First Printing June 2001
Printed in Korea

Publisher's Cataloging-in-Publication

Levy, Kimberley M.
    Chelsea's new home / by Kimberley M. Levy ;
illustrated by Terry Herman. -- 1st ed.
    p. cm.
    SUMMARY: Colorful rhyming story of an adventurous
goldfish who teaches children to pursue their dreams.
    LCCN 2001-086177
    ISBN 0-9706531-2-3

    1. Goldfish--Juvenile fiction. 2. Courage--Juvenile
fiction. [1. Goldfish--Fiction. 2. Courage--Fiction.
3. Stories in rhyme.] I. Herman, Terry. II. Title.

PZ8.3.L575Che 2001   [E]
                     QBI01-700181

www.chelseasnewhome.com

Published by PB Publishing,
a division of Printstar Books, Milwaukee, Wisconsin

PRINTSTAR
BOOKS★

5630 N. Lake Drive, Milwaukee, Wisconsin 53217
414-906-0600 • e-mail: pbpub@execpc.com

Affiliated Publishers
Milwaukee • Denver • Vancouver, B.C.

For my mother, Bobbie Gerol, who taught me courage and who continues to give me endless support. You were the best.

— KML

For Pat, who is beautiful in every way.

— Terry

Chelsea Fish swam for hours
among the red and yellow flowers
as she played with her friends Lou
and Marianne and Betty Sue.

An artificial pond was her home,

made of sleek and shiny chrome,

in the window of a store

that sold flowers, plants, and more.

But Chelsea pined to have more fun,
to watch a real setting sun,
to feel fresh air upon her fins
and the force of blustery winds.
Chelsea dreamed of what lay beyond
her same old artificial pond.

Every day, Florist Joe

stood beneath the portico

to stretch his legs and get fresh air

and rearrange his outdoor ware.

One day while Chelsea Fish watched Joe,

she knew she simply had to go!

Chelsea splashed a fin and gave a cry,
"The time has come to say goodbye
to this pond that's been my home
and follow my heart's dream to roam."

She sped to ask her friends Lou

and Marianne and Betty Sue

if they would like to come along

to find a home where they'd belong.

She told her friends of all her dreams
to sleep by the glow of white moonbeams.
Her sparkling eyes were filled with glee,
"Please say you'll come away with me!"

The friends just stared at Chelsea Fish.

They had never had a wish

to leave the safety of the store

or see the world beyond the door.

So they wished Chelsea all the best.

"Good luck to you on your quest,

and even if you go away,

we're sure to meet again someday!"

After her friends had gone to bed,
plans of escape filled Chelsea's head.
By the time of the next day's dawn,
her final plan was fully drawn.

Right on cue the truck arrived.

The shop went into overdrive

with flowers going in and out.

"This is my chance to break out!"

As Joe returned the unsold fronds,

he passed the artificial pond.

Chelsea seized her chance to escape

and leapt onto the sticky tape

dangling from the box of flowers.

These few seconds seemed like hours.

She marveled that she could be so bold
but wondered what the future might hold.
Yet Chelsea couldn't keep from grinning.
Her new life was just beginning.

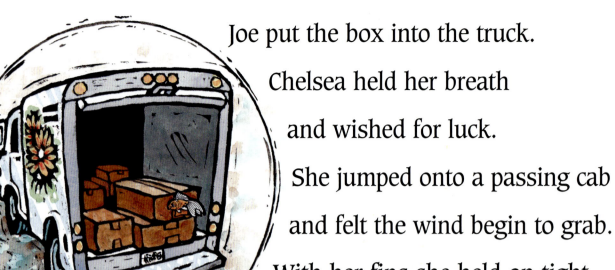

Joe put the box into the truck.

Chelsea held her breath

and wished for luck.

She jumped onto a passing cab

and felt the wind begin to grab.

With her fins she held on tight,

clutching now with all her might.

She looked up at the wide, blue sky.

She nodded to a butterfly.

Chelsea saw fantastic sights—
planes and clouds and high-flying kites!

Chelsea had done it! She was free at last!

Then suddenly, she felt a blast

of cold, strong wind. Chelsea let go.

She sailed into a movie show.

What was this place so drab and dark?

On the screen she saw a shark!

"Oh, no!" small Chelsea cried with fear.

"How do I get out of here?"

Out the door she flew in a flash
and landed in a pile of trash.
It was too smelly for her to take.
From tail to fin she began to shake.
Chelsea bravely forced a smile.
"Finding a home might take awhile."

Chelsea started down the street.

Odd creatures she began to meet.

First a hairy four-legged thing

whose gaze she felt was menacing.

Chelsea quickly stepped aside

so she wouldn't land inside

its big and ugly drippy mouth.

Chelsea turned and headed south.

"That was close," she thought with relief.

Then her eyes widened in disbelief.

Zooming toward her, what was that?

In an orange and purple hat,

rolled a monster made of wood

on top of which a giant stood.

Chelsea sprung to a flower spray

and watched the skateboard coast away.

When out of nowhere came a shot
of dust and dirt and old dry rot.
A street sweeper had gone by,
throwing grime into the sky.

The dusty film coated Chelsea.

And that is when she wished to be

back in her artificial pond,

back among the big, green fronds.

Chelsea slowly flapped away.

With her friends she longed to play.

Then Chelsea sniffed a familiar smell,

a smell she knew so very well.

The smell of water, grass—ALGAE!

From where it came, she could not see.

Chelsea walked faster, led by her nose,

forgetting quickly her recent woes.

Around a corner, past a tree…

"I'm getting close," she said hopefully.

Then she saw water—crystal blue.

"My dream of home is coming true."

All around was grass so tall.

There even was a waterfall.

Chelsea's heart began to soar.

"This is just what I've been looking for!"

Chelsea dove into her brand-new home

from which she knew she'd never roam.

"This is where I'm meant to be,
in a natural pond and FREE!"